A Royal Robber

Written by Karen Wallace
Illustrated by Cathy Brett

WAYLAND

Princess PJ was a tomboy. She loved riding horses more than anything else in the world.

She could gallop faster and jump higher than any prince in the land. But PJ had no one to ride with. She had to ride all by herself.

Her brother, Prince Dandyfop, thought horses were scary.

Her mother, Queen Clementine, thought horses were smelly.

Her father, King Crusty, liked horses, but he was very forgetful. He would put on his riding clothes and go swimming instead!

One day Princess PJ was riding alone in the forest.

Suddenly a man in a mask galloped up to her. He was carrying an enormous water pistol.

"Give me your carrots," he demanded.
"Or I'll zap you with my water pistol!"

Princess PJ burst out laughing.
"Carrots? Why do you want carrots?
What kind of robber are you?"

"A good robber!" cried the man. "I steal
from the rich to give to the poor."

"Why do poor people need carrots?" asked Princess PJ.
"To make soup, of course," said the robber. "Everyone knows poor people eat lots of soup."

He held up a sack. "I've already got onions, potatoes and meaty bones. Now hand over your carrots."

"I don't have any carrots, but you can have my pocket money."

Princess PJ reached into her pocket and held out some coins.

"What good is that?" asked the robber.
"Poor people can't eat money."

"They can buy things with it," replied Princess PJ. "And they might want a change from soup."

"You're right," said the robber thoughtfully. "It is boring to eat soup all the time."

Princess PJ had a brilliant idea. "Empty that sack and come with me," she cried. "I want to help poor people, too!"

18

Princess PJ took the robber home.
On the way, she told him the story of
Robin Hood and how he stole gold and
silver from rich people and gave it to
poor people.

"Then what happened?" asked the
robber, who had never heard the story.

"Everyone lived happily ever after,"
said Princess PJ. "Now, here we are.
Tie up your horse and follow me."

23

The robber stared in amazement.
"But this is a palace!" he cried.

"That's because I am a princess," replied Princess PJ. "Follow me and do as I say."

An hour later, Princess PJ led the robber back to his horse.

His sack was bulging with silver
candlesticks, gold plates, sparkling
jewels and all the coins from Princess
PJ's piggy bank.

"But what about the king and queen?"
asked the robber. "Won't they
be cross?"

"Oh, my father won't notice, and my mother loves an excuse to go shopping for new things," replied Princess PJ. Her eyes twinkled.

"Good luck," laughed Princess PJ,
"and remember the story. Everyone
lives happily ever after!"

START READING is a series of highly enjoyable books for beginner readers. **The books have been carefully graded to match the Book Bands widely used in schools.** This enables readers to be sure they choose books that match their own reading ability.

Look out for the Band colour on the book in our Start Reading logo.

The Bands are:

	Pink Band 1
	Red Band 2
	Yellow Band 3
	Blue Band 4
	Green Band 5
	Orange Band 6
	Turquoise Band 7
	Purple Band 8
	Gold Band 9

START READING books can be read independently or shared with an adult. They promote the enjoyment of reading through satisfying stories supported by fun illustrations.

Karen Wallace was brought up in a log cabin in Canada. She has written lots of different books for children and even won a few awards. Karen likes writing funny books because she can laugh at her own jokes! She has two sons and two cats.

Cathy Brett has been scribbling all her life – first on pieces of paper, on walls and sometimes on her sister! She later became a fashion designer and an author/illustrator. Her scribbles have appeared in lots of books, in shop windows and even on beach towels. Cathy likes listening to really loud rock music!